KOOKS in the Cafeteria

Thanks, Janet Kusmierski,
for making everything look great!
—T.R.

ISBN-13: 978-0-545-00399-5
ISBN-10: 0-545-00399-7

12 11 10 9 8 7 6 5 4   8 9 10 11 12 13/0

Printed in the U.S.A.
First printing, January 2008

Comic Guy

KOOKS in the Cafeteria

BY TIMOTHY ROLAND

Scholastic Inc.
New York Toronto London Auckland Sydney
Mexico City New Delhi Hong Kong Buenos Aires

CHAPTER ONE

WHAT'S THE PLAN?

It's not true that math word problems are good for nothing. Because they're good for putting me to sleep. That's what happened on Friday. Math class went—

from boring . . .   to me snoring . . .

to Mr. Crane sending me to face something even tougher than a math word problem, and tougher than the school cafeteria's food.

He sent me to face the principal.

"Life isn't fair!" I said as I stepped into the office.

Miss Little, the principal's secretary, looked at me and grinned. "Weren't you just here yesterday, Guy?"

"Yes," I mumbled. "And the day before that, and the day before that. But what happened wasn't my fault!"

"Of course not," chuckled Miss Little. She pointed to a chair with my name on it. "He'll be with you in a minute, so take a seat."

I sat down, pulled out my sketchbook, and worked on a **COMIC GUY** comic strip. I write and illustrate it for the school newspaper. It's about me, and about what happens at school.

I laughed, until I heard—

"Maloney!"

"Yes, Mr. Crane...I mean, yes Principal Hawk." I looked up at his snarling bulldog face, then followed him into his office.

To Principal Hawk, school was serious business. Which meant—

— No laughing in school.

— No funny stuff in school.

— No eating candy in school (except for him).

glaring eyes

grouchy face

candy filled stomach

He sat behind his desk like the judge at my trial. Then he snatched the piece of paper I was holding. "Hmm. This note from Mr. Crane says you were sleeping in his class! Is it true?"

His glare hit me hard. But I was ready— with Plan A.

"Yes, Principal Hawk," I replied. "But I've already been punished for it."

The principal's eyebrows shot upward.

"Education is valuable," I explained. "So by sleeping in class, I punished myself by missing some of my valuable education."

Principal Hawk scratched his head.

Perfect. He was confused. And I was on a roll. Unfortunately, I kept rolling.

"I only hurt myself by what I did," I said. "And I wasn't bothering anyone else."

"But this note says you were snoring!"

Oops! I had forgotten. Which meant it was time to switch to Plan B.

"But it wasn't my fault I fell asleep," I explained, trying to look innocent.

I wonder if Mr. Crane ever bored himself to sleep.

"And whose fault was it?"

"Mr. Crane's."

"Mr. Crane's?!"

8

"Well, not entirely Mr. Crane's fault," I said, realizing I had to be careful. "He can't help that he teaches math, which at times can make students...sleepy."

Principal Hawk leaned forward and scowled. "So you're telling me Mr. Crane's math class was so boring that it put you to sleep?"

"Well, not exactly," I replied, seeing that he wasn't buying it.

"So whose fault was it?" demanded a glaring Principal Hawk.

I gulped hard. I needed an answer—FAST! But all I could think to say was . . .

"Mashed potatoes," I said again as Plan C popped into my head. "You've eaten the cafeteria's mashed potatoes, haven't you?" I asked Principal Hawk.

"Yes."

"And you know how heavy they are?"

The principal nodded and cracked a small grin. So did I, as I thought about the mashed potatoes.

HOW HEAVY ARE THEY?

A bowl of the school's mashed potatoes.

"Well, I have math class right after lunch," I explained. "And today I was served an extra large portion of mashed potatoes, which sat in my stomach like a rock and made me feel very, very sleepy."

"Hmmm." Principal Hawk rubbed his chin. "I think I understand."

"You do?"

"Yes," answered the principal. "It was the kitchen's fault."

"So I'm off the hook?" I asked, smiling.

"Not exactly. You're still guilty of sleeping in class. But because of the circumstances, I don't think detention would be the appropriate punishment."

I let out a sigh of relief.

"Instead, I'm sentencing you to K.P. duty."

"Huh?" I said.

"One week of working in the school kitchen!" Principal Hawk slammed his fist on his desk like a judge pounding his gavel.

BAM!

The case was closed.

And I was right.

SOMETIMES LIFE JUST ISN'T FAIR!

THE BARKER

Rockyville Elementary School News

KID SENT TO WOLF

Guy Maloney was sentenced to one week of working in the school kitchen. Starting Monday, he will be under the command of the rarely-seen head cook, (the big bad) Mrs. Wolf.

When asked if he was worried about going into the kitchen, Guy paused for a moment, then nodded. "Although," he said, "I'm much more worried about coming out . . . alive!"

WHAT DO YOU MEAN YOU'RE BEING PUNISHED?! I'M THE ONE WHO WILL BE PREPARING FOOD IN THE KITCHEN.

GUY MALONEY

AND WE'RE THE ONES WHO WILL HAVE TO EAT IT.

CHAPTER TWO

THE FUNNY SIDE

On Monday, I grabbed a clothespin and headed off to school with Molly.

"This is going to be exciting, Guy," she said.

"Exciting?!" I glanced at Molly. She was my neighbor, my best friend, and at the moment, out of her mind. "You ever get a whiff of the school kitchen?" I asked.

Molly held her nose.

I snapped the clothes-pin onto mine.

"You need to look on the bright side, Guy," said Molly.

I was ready.

"You mean," I said, "I need to look on the funny side." Which is how I get ideas for my comic strip. Fortunately, lots of funny stuff happens at Rockyville Elementary School. Like in last Friday's math class.

I FINISHED ALL BUT ONE OF THE MATH HOMEWORK PROBLEMS, MOLLY. GUESS WHICH ONE?

GUY MALONEY, WOULD YOU PLEASE SOLVE PROBLEM NINE AT THE BOARD.

THAT ONE.

GUY MALONEY

BEING STARED AT WHILE STANDING IN FRONT OF THE WHOLE CLASS AFFECTS MY MEMORY.

SO YOU'RE SAYING YOU FORGOT HOW TO SOLVE PROBLEM NUMBER NINE?

GUY MALONEY

NO. I'M SAYING I FORGOT WHAT PROBLEM NUMBER NINE EVEN IS.

IF YOU DRIVE A CAR AT 60 MILES PER HOUR FOR 30 MINUTES, THEN AT 30 MILES PER HOUR FOR 60 MINUTES, HOW FAR WILL YOU TRAVEL?

WELL, WHAT'S YOUR ANSWER, GUY?

ZERO MILES. BECAUSE I'M TOO YOUNG TO DRIVE.

GUY MALONEY

"And that's how I got into this mess," I moaned as I kept walking.

"Me, too," said Molly.

"What?"

Molly smiled. "I've been sentenced to work in the school kitchen with you."

"You have? But why?"

"Because we're pals," replied Molly as she

slapped me on the back. "Which means we do things together."

"And now," I sighed, "we'll be working in the school kitchen together."

"You didn't think I was going to let you have fun all alone, did you?" said Molly as she began walking faster.

"Fun? In the kitchen? Are you crazy?!"

Molly grinned. "Just think of it as an adventure filled with challenges, discoveries, and rewards." As I raced to keep up, I thought about her words.

Okay, it did sound like fun. Which is why I raced Molly to school. And why my heart thumped with excitement. And why I smiled extra wide, until the kitchen door swung open and a grouchy voice yelled out, "Get in here! And get to work!"

CHAPTER THREE

TWO KOOKS

There was only one thing in the kitchen scarier than yesterday's leftovers. And me and Molly were looking at her.

— Six feet tall

— Wide as a refrigerator

— Glaring eyes nasty enough to make milk turn sour (and make my knees shake with fear)

"It's about time you two kids got here!"
roared Mrs. Wolf while stomping closer. She
yanked us into the smelly kitchen, shut the
door, and tossed us each an apron.

I put mine on, snapped on my clothespin,
and looked around.

At the messy tables.

At the pots and pans.

At someone buried beneath a pile of work.

"Look at me when I'm talking to you!"
ordered Mrs. Wolf. She snatched away my
clothespin and glared. "There'll be no fooling
around in my kitchen! Or else!"

Sweat dripped down my neck as she
smacked her hands together and glared at me
like...well, like the Big Bad Wolf.

"Lunch is in three hours!" she roared. "So get it ready!" She marched to her office and—BAM!—slammed the door.

The walls shook.

The pots on the table rattled.

"So what do we do now?" I asked.

"Explore!" replied Molly.

"But Mrs. Wolf said—"

"I know," interrupted Molly. She yanked my arm. "Come on, Guy!"

Molly led me toward the large pile of pots, pans, and food. Underneath, working hard, was the assistant cook, Miss Beany.

"So why are you in the kitchen?" asked Miss Beany.

"It's part of Principal Hawk's new system of discipline," I explained, "where the punishment must fit the crime."

"The crime?"

"Don't ask," I sighed.

"Well, whatever the reason, I'm glad you're here," said Miss Beany while continuing to work. "Because the Food Inspector is coming some time this week. And there's lots for us to do."

"Doesn't Mrs. Wolf help?" I asked, glancing at the closed office door.

Miss Beany lowered her tired eyes and shook her head. "No."

"But that's not fair!" I said.

"You're right. But this week it doesn't matter. Because this week, you and Molly are here to help." She grinned at us like we were the cavalry riding in to save the day.

Unfortunately, I didn't know anything about riding a horse—or about working in a kitchen. Which meant Miss Beany was in for an unpleasant surprise.

And, as I was about to find out, so was I.

CHAPTER FOUR

HELP?

"We must move fast, because there's lots to do," said Miss Beany. She scampered across the kitchen like a nervous hen, climbed a stepladder, and dove into her work. (But fortunately, not into the large pot of soup she was preparing for lunch.)

"Mrs. Wolf wants you two to get this ready," said Miss Beany. She tossed Molly a card.

"What is it?" I asked.

"A recipe," answered Molly, showing me the card.

"With lots of words and numbers," I groaned. It reminded me of a math word problem, which reminded me of a dragon—because both are nearly impossible to conquer!

math word problem   me

I looked closer at the card. It was a recipe for 200 servings of chocolate pudding. "But we're supposed to make enough for 500 students," I said to Molly.

"Then we'll need to use more of the ingredients," she replied.

"How much more?"

Molly shrugged.

I looked again at the card. Doing math made me sleepy. Which is why I came up with a plan.

Before Molly had a chance to argue, I was across the kitchen, standing in front of the supply room, and grinning. It was the perfect plan. No math for me! Instead, I'd be getting supplies, which I knew would be much easier.

Until I heard the noise.

28

"I tried to stop him from taking the cookies," said Tank.

"Did not!" I said as cookie crumbs tumbled from my mouth.

Mrs. Wolf glanced at me, then at Tank. She patted him on the head. "Good boy! Now scram!"

"But this isn't what it looks like," I argued.

"I'll be the judge of that! And I say…"

YOU'RE GUILTY!

Mrs. Wolf threw some supplies into my hands and shoved me back into the kitchen. "And for punishment," she scolded, "you will prepare the dessert…alone!"

"But where's Molly?" I asked.

"Preparing the vegetables."

"And Miss Beany?"

"Cooking the soup."

"And what will you be doing?"

Mrs. Wolf shot me a fiery glare. "None of your business! Now get to work!" She marched into her office and—BAM!—slammed the door.

The kitchen shook.

So did my hands as I picked up the recipe card.

Chocolate Pudding

1. Mix 5 pounds of pudding powder with 6 gallons of milk.
2. Cook until mixture comes to a boil.
3. Pour into bowls and refrigerate.

Recipe makes 200 servings.

But I needed to figure out how much of the ingredients to use to make 500 servings. Which meant...

I poured some chocolate pudding powder into a large pot. I added milk. Then more milk. And more milk. And to make sure I made enough pudding, I continued adding milk until Miss Beany came over to check on my progress.

"Is it ready?" she asked.

"I think so."

She lifted the pot onto the stove, cooked it, and helped me pour the watery brown liquid into small bowls. Then she told me to stick the bowls in the refrigerator to chill until we served lunch.

HOW DID THE PUDDING TURN OUT, GUY?

IT LOOKS LIKE SOUP.

BUT MAYBE NO ONE WILL NOTICE.

But they did.

THE BARKER

Rockyville Elementary School News

KID COOKS UP MISTAKE

Guy Maloney, a kitchen helper for the week, has created a new student favorite —chocolate soup. "I was trying to prepare pudding," explained Guy, "but made a mistake."

Mrs. Wolf, the head cook, agreed. "Of course it was a mistake. Because the only thing Guy knows how to cook up is trouble."

CONGRATULATIONS ON YOUR CHOCOLATE SOUP, GUY.

THANKS.

SO WHAT ARE YOU PLANNING TO MAKE NEXT?

GUY MALONEY

BESIDES A MESS.

CHAPTER FIVE

WHAT'S THE BUZZ?

Tuesday morning, I flew into the beehive (which is what I called the newspaper room). Like usual, it was buzzing with activity. And in the center of the confusion stood Zoe, the queen bee, shouting out orders.

I moved slowly toward Zoe. She looked grouchy, annoyed, angry. In other words, she looked like her normal self.

"This should cheer you up," I said. I handed her a comic strip.

MRS. WOLF IS BOTH A COOK AND A MAGICIAN.

WHY DO YOU SAY THAT, GUY?

BECAUSE THE FOOD SHE SERVES MAKES MY APPETITE DISAPPEAR.

GUY MALONEY

I laughed.

Zoe groaned. "Get serious, Maloney!" she snarled. "Because what our school newspaper needs is—"

"Help!" said a voice behind me.

I watched as Zapper stepped in front of Zoe. "I need help doing my job," he said.

"Are you kidding?" sneered Zoe.

"Nope." He unzipped his backpack and out jumped Ollie, the science class pet monkey. "And I was hoping you'd let Ollie join the newspaper staff as my assistant."

"Forget it!"

Zapper paused, thought, and grinned. "Well then, how about if he does my job and I

35

become *his* assistant?"

Zoe's face turned red. Her hands tightened into fists. "Just get to work!" she ordered. Which is what Zapper did.

He had a very important job.

Because he (and Ollie) delivered the paper.

Zoe slapped her head as she watched them head into the hallway. "See what I have to work with," she mumbled. "So how am I ever going to make this a better newspaper?"

"Add more comic strips." I chuckled.

"But this is supposed to be a serious newspaper!"

"Says who?"

Zoe clenched her teeth and shot me a fiery glare.

"And except for Principal Hawk." An evil grin slithered onto Zoe's face as she pointed her nose directly at me. "And he told me that I could fire anyone on the newspaper staff who doesn't do their job."

"But I do my job. See." I pointed to my comic strip. "I'm the cartoonist."

"Well, now you're also a reporter."

"I am?"

Zoe tossed me a small reporter's notebook. "And you're going to find out what our readers want to know about the school kitchen."

"No. Something even bigger," said Zoe.

"Like what?" I asked.

"That's what you're going to find out."

"How?"

"Investigate."

"And if I don't come up with anything?"

"Then you haven't done your job," said Zoe, grinning. "And you'll be fired."

"What? You can't do that!"

"According to Principal Hawk, I can," said Zoe, buzzing like a bee. "And if you're not on the newspaper staff, you can't contribute to the newspaper."

"But—"

Zoe had been searching for a way to get rid of **COMIC GUY**. And this was it!

"But that's not fair!" I argued.

Zoe's evil grin widened. "You have until the end of this week," she said as she pointed to the door.

I glanced at her, and at the **COMIC GUY** comic strip on her desk. Then I shuffled out of the beehive and headed slowly back to the smelly kitchen, where I began looking for a story. But all I found was the big bad Mrs. Wolf.

And more trouble.

CHAPTER SIX

A (TOO) HOT IDEA

Okay, I had a problem to solve. I needed to find a newspaper story. Something big. And the biggest thing I saw when I stepped into the kitchen was Mrs. Wolf barreling toward me.

Her steaming head looked hot enough to cook on.

"Yesterday was a disaster!" she shouted.

"Yesterday?" I paused as I thought about what had happened.

"So what are you grinning about, Maloney?" she snarled.

"Nothing," I lied. Although actually, I was thinking about yesterday, when...

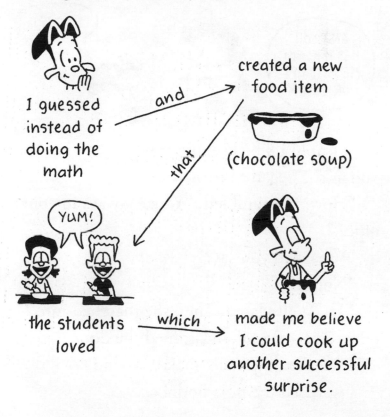

I guessed instead of doing the math **and** created a new food item (chocolate soup) **that** the students loved **which** made me believe I could cook up another successful surprise.

YUM!

"So you think you're something special, do you?" asked Mrs. Wolf.

I shrugged…and grinned.

"Well, we'll see about that." Mrs. Wolf slapped a recipe card into my hands. "Because today, you're going to prepare the main course. Alone!"

"Hmph! I'll be keeping my eye on you," she said as she began to turn.

"How?" I mumbled. "You're always in your office."

"What did you say?"

"Nothing."

Mrs. Wolf glared. Then she marched into her office and—BAM!—slammed the door.

I watched the walls shake.

I watched the pots bounce.

Then, in my mind, I saw it—the newspaper story I was looking for. Something big. Something dangerous. I would investigate why Mrs. Wolf didn't help in the kitchen.

But first, I had work to do. I looked at the recipe card.

Tuna Surprise

1. Mix 12 pounds of tuna, 8 gallons of milk, 6 bags of noodles, 3 pounds of butter, 2 pounds of chopped celery, 2 pounds of flour, 1 pound of salt.
2. Bake at 300 degrees for 30 minutes.

Recipe makes 250 servings.

"No problem," I said. "Except that I need to make 500 servings. Which means I have to do some math."

"Did somebody say 'math'?"

I turned as a blur circled me twice, then screeched to a stop.

"Math word problems are easy," explained Clint. "Just break them into pieces."

I scratched my head. "You mean, cut them down to size?"

"Exactly."

A MATH WORD PROBLEM

... CUT DOWN TO SIZE.

Clint grinned, then looked at the recipe card. "This recipe makes 250 servings. But you need to make enough for 500, which is twice as much as 250. So you must multiply the ingredient amounts by two."

"So instead of using 12 pounds of tuna," I said, "I should use 24 pounds?"

"Exactly."

"And instead of 8 gallons of milk, I should use 16 gallons?"

Clint smiled. "Now you're getting it."

"Yeah," I said, smiling back, "I am. Thanks."

"No problem." Clint spun around.

"So what brings you to the kitchen?" I asked before he blasted off.

"I delivered our classroom's lunch money," answered Clint. "And I wanted to see the school's star cook in action." He grinned, spun his wheels, and in a flash, was gone.

I looked again at the recipe card. I multiplied the ingredients by two, mixed them all together, and poured them into several pans. I set the pans in the oven and watched Miss Beany turn the temperature to 300 degrees.

Then, I got an idea.

IT'S SUPPOSED TO BAKE AT 300° FOR 30 MINUTES.

BUT IF YOU TURN THE OVEN TO 600° (TWICE AS HIGH), IT SHOULD TAKE ONLY 15 MINUTES (HALF AS LONG).

And that's what I did.

It was brilliant. The math was right. "And," I said after scooting over to where Molly was working, "it will make preparing lunch go faster. Which will give us time to explore and find out why Mrs. Wolf stays in her office."

"Good idea," said Molly.

"You mean, brilliant idea," I said. Then, I smiled—until I smelled the smoke. And I saw Miss Beany point toward the oven. And I heard her yell...

FIRE!

CHAPTER SEVEN

BURNED!

"FIRE! FIRE!"

Miss Beany scampered toward the oven, flapping her arms in the air and squawking like a rooster at sunrise. "FIRE! FIRE!"

But she was wrong.

Because when she yanked open the oven door, I didn't see fire—only smoke. Lots and lots of thick black smoke, which poured into the smelly kitchen air.

SEE WHAT YOU DID BY TURNING ON THE OVEN TOO HIGH, GUY?

ACTUALLY, MISS BEANY, I CAN'T SEE ANYTHING AT ALL.

GUY MALONEY

"Get some water!" yelled Miss Beany.

Molly and I bumped into pots, pans, and

48

tables as we raced across the kitchen. We each filled a bucket with water. Then, half-squinting, we bumped our way back to the oven.

Molly unloaded her bucket—SPLASH!—into the oven. It spit back a dark cloud of smoke, and for a moment, I couldn't see. But I tossed my water anyway. And I hit—

I stepped back as the smoke cleared.

"Isn't she supposed to melt?" whispered Molly.

"Huh?" I said.

"Like in *The Wizard of Oz*...the Wicked Witch."

I smiled a little. Then—WHOOSH!—Mrs. Wolf yanked me off my feet and shook me like she was making a milkshake.

For a moment, all I saw was a blur. But when the shaking stopped, I could see water still dripping down Mrs. Wolf's fiery-hot face. Then I looked over at the Tuna Surprise. It was black, hard, and still smoking.

"But it's ruined!" screamed Mrs. Wolf.

"And lunch is in half an hour!" squawked Miss Beany. "And the Food Inspector could be coming...today!"

"Then you'll need to prepare a new meal." Mrs. Wolf glared at me, at Molly, at Miss Beany.

"And what do you suggest?" asked Miss Beany.

"That you think of something quickly. And that you get to work on it right away!" Mrs. Wolf turned, marched into her office, and— BAM!—slammed her door.

"Why doesn't she help?" I asked, glancing from the closed office door to Miss Beany.

She shrugged.

"But it isn't fair!"

"Baloney!" said Miss Beany.

"What?"

"Baloney!" she said again. Then she scampered to the supply room and returned with a pile of sliced meat. "We'll make baloney sand- wiches," she said, grinning. Which is what the three of us did.

BALONEY!

Fortunately, we didn't get a visit from the Food Inspector. But when the lunch bell rang, the first person in line was a hungry-looking Principal Hawk.

THE BARKER

Rockyville Elementary School News

LUNCH GETS FIRED

Smoke billowed through the kitchen after Guy Maloney burned the Tuna Surprise. "I accidentally turned the oven on too high," he explained, "and the food caught fire."

"But fortunately," said head cook Mrs. Wolf, "there was enough time to replace the lunch with baloney sandwiches. Because the Tuna Surprise didn't survive. And I doubt that Guy will, either."

TODAY I FOUND OUT THAT PRINCIPAL HAWK'S FAVORITE FOOD IS A BALONEY SANDWICH.

REALLY?

GUY MALONEY

WHICH EXPLAINS WHY HE'S USUALLY FULL OF BALONEY.

CHAPTER EIGHT

IT'S ABOUT TIME

Unfortunately, Zoe had a different opinion when she confronted me in the beehive on Wednesday morning. "Say good-bye to **COMIC GUY**," she announced.

"Why?" I looked at her holding yesterday's edition of the newspaper.

"I don't like this comic strip," she replied. "And neither does Principal Hawk."

"Because I said he's full of baloney? But everyone knows that's true."

Zoe didn't argue.

"And you said if I uncover a big story about

the kitchen, you'd keep **COMIC GUY** in the
newspaper." I grabbed her copy. I pointed to
the story about the fire.

I flipped open my reporter's notebook.
"But I'm working on another big story."

"About what?"

"About why the head cook, Mrs. Wolf,
always disappears into her office and doesn't
help prepare the food."

Zoe's eyes widened. "So what's the answer?"

"I don't know yet."

"Why not?" Zoe stepped closer and glared.

I stepped back, then explained. "It's because
in the kitchen—"

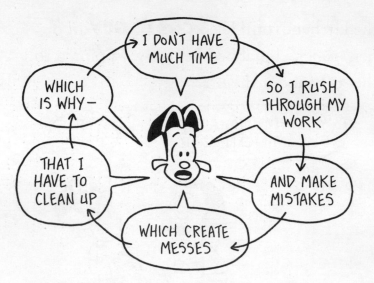

"Then make some time!" ordered Zoe. "Or else!"

Unfortunately, Wednesday was one of those days when it was harder to make time than it was to make food.

Do the
math.

Peel the
potatoes.

Chop the
vegetables.

Get the
chicken.

Mix the
broth.

OOPS!

Clean
up.

Do it all
again.

Ready to
serve.

58

COMIC GUY WAYS OF SERVING CAFETERIA FOOD

The "I-Hear-Nothing" approach.

The catch of the day.

Feeding the "I can't wait to eat" kid.

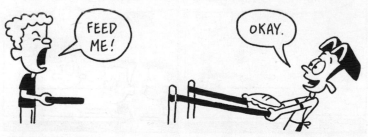

YOU DROPPED YOUR TRAY ON PURPOSE?!

YEP.

AND THERE'S NOTHING YOU CAN DO ABOUT IT.

BUT I CAN.

GUY MALONEY

WHY ISN'T TANK'S MESS BEING CLEANED UP?

IT WILL BE.

...BY OUR NEW JANITOR'S HELPER FOR THE WEEK.

GUY MALONEY

CHAPTER NINE
PLAN B (CAREFUL)

On Thursday morning, it was hard to crawl out of bed. It was even harder to shuffle to school. But the hardest thing I had to do was look at the sneering face of the big bad Mrs. Wolf.

"Here's lunch! Get it ready!" She tossed me a recipe card, then disappeared into her office.

"It's not fair that she doesn't help," I grumbled. "And today I'm going to find out why."

"So what's our plan, Guy?" asked Molly. I could tell from her gigantic grin that she was ready for action.

"We get cooking," I replied.

"Huh?"

"You slice and butter the bread, and I'll make the spaghetti sauce."

"But what about—"

"One problem at a time," I said as I studied my recipe card and began working out the math. Then I mixed the ingredients in a pot and handed it to Miss Beany to cook on the stove.

"Now we can explore," I said to Molly as I led the way toward Mrs. Wolf's closed office door.

WHAT'S THE MAIN GOAL OF OUR MISSION, GUY?

TO GET INTO MRS. WOLF'S OFFICE? TO FIND OUT WHAT SHE'S DOING?

TO NOT GET CAUGHT.

"So how do we get into the big bad Mrs. Wolf's office?" asked Molly. "Huff, puff, and blow the door down?" She chuckled.

So did I. "Actually," I said, "we get in by you knocking on the door."

Molly laughed harder.

"I'm serious," I explained. "It's part of my 'hide-and-peek' plan."

"Think it will work?" asked Molly.

"Of course," I replied, trying to sound confident. Although as I hid behind some boxes, I pictured in my mind what would happen if it didn't.

"Ready, Guy?" asked Molly.

I nodded.

"Okay," she warned, "here goes." She knocked. And knocked. And knocked. "Looks like nobody's home."

"You sure?"

Molly nodded. "And look—the door's not locked." She turned the handle and slowly pushed it open so we could see what was inside Mrs. Wolf's office.

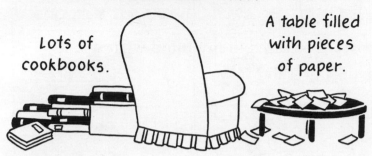

The back of a comfortable chair.

Lots of cookbooks.

A table filled with pieces of paper.

Molly tiptoed toward the table. "Look at all those numbers," she whispered.

I moved slowly (and carefully) closer. I looked at the papers. They were filled with numbers—food quantities, temperatures, number of kids who bought hot lunches. And they all needed to be added, subtracted, multiplied, or divided, and then written onto recipe cards.

"Whew! If I had to do all that math," I said, "I'd get very, very sleepy."

"Me, too," said Molly. She stretched her arms in the air and faked a yawn.

I chuckled for a moment, until—

CHAPTER TEN
I DON'T BELIEVE IT!

Friday morning, I walked with Molly toward the kitchen. "You sick, Guy?" she asked.

"No. Why?"

"Because we're headed into the kitchen— and you're smiling!"

"That's because I wrote the story about Mrs. Wolf and Zoe is reading it right now. And **COMIC GUY** will be staying in the school paper—probably forever!"

"I hope you're right," said Molly. She pointed over my shoulder toward Zoe, who was steaming our way.

"And no one else will believe it, either!" roared Zoe. "Which is why I can't print it in the newspaper." She tossed it onto the floor.

"But the story's true!" I argued.

"Prove it!"

"I have a witness," I said, pointing at Molly. We turned and stared at her.

ACTUALLY, I'M NOT SURE I BELIEVE WHAT HAPPENED, EITHER.

"See what I mean, Maloney!" snarled Zoe. She stepped closer and glared. "You can't go around making up lies about teachers!"

"But it isn't a lie," I said. "And Mrs. Wolf isn't a teacher."

"Hmph!" Zoe's hair swished through the air as she spun around. "Just get me a real story before the end of the day... or you can say good-bye to **COMIC GUY**."

She flashed
an evil
crocodile
smile.

I watched her walk toward class. But in my mind, I was watching my comic strip being kicked out of the newspaper. Then I stepped into the kitchen and stared at Molly. "What do you mean, you don't believe what happened?!"

Molly shrugged. "Do you?"

But before I could answer, a crashing noise shot out of the refrigerated supply room.

"It's probably Tank again," I mumbled.

"What?" asked Molly.

"I said, it's probably a big rat."

"Really? A rat?" Molly grinned. "I always wanted a pet rat."

"Not this rat," I warned. But before I had a chance to explain, Molly grabbed a big pot and rushed into the supply room.

I followed carefully.

Tank escaped. Molly and I froze as if our feet were stuck in cement.

"What are you doing in here?!" roared the big bad Mrs. Wolf. Her glare was hot enough to toast bread (or a kid she caught misbehaving).

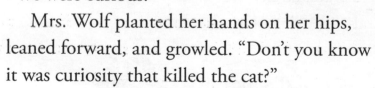

"We were just looking around," I answered nervously. "We were curious."

Mrs. Wolf planted her hands on her hips, leaned forward, and growled. "Don't you know it was curiosity that killed the cat?"

"I thought it was the school food she ate," joked Molly.

We both laughed.

Mrs. Wolf nearly exploded.

Fortunately, just then Miss Beany raced in. "The Food Inspector is coming today!" she warned. "And there's lots to do to get lunch ready."

"Then do it!" Mrs. Wolf pushed us all back into the kitchen.

"But we're supposed to serve hamburgers," said Miss Beany. "And we don't have enough meat to make burgers for everyone."

Mrs. Wolf raised her evil eyebrows. "Well then, it looks like you have a problem to solve," she said in an icy voice. Then she turned and glared at me and Molly as if to say, "I'll deal with you two later!"

I watched her march into her office and—BAM!—slam the door.

IT'S NOT FAIR!

"No, it's not," moaned Miss Beany.

"And I'm going to do something about it!" I promised.

"What?" asked Molly.

I looked at her. I looked at the nervous Miss Beany. I had no idea what I was going to do. "I'll come up with something...later," I said. "Because right now we have—"

CHAPTER ELEVEN

BALONEY!

"We have enough meat to make 400 hamburgers," stated Miss Beany. "But we need to figure out how to make at least 500."

So I went fishing for ideas, and—

"So what's your idea, Guy?" asked Molly.

LEMONADE.

WHAT?

"We make lemonade," I said.

Molly scratched her head. "Are you crazy?!"

"Yes. I mean, no. I mean—" I looked at Molly, at Miss Beany, then I explained. "My dad told me that when life hands us lemons, we should make lemonade."

"But lemonade's not on the menu," said Miss Beany.

I chuckled. "What he meant was that when we run into problems, we should do the best we can with what we have."

"And what do we have?" asked Miss Beany.

"My idea."

"But we need more meat!"

"Or something to mix with it so we can make enough hamburgers." I led the way into the refrigerated supply room, grinned, and pointed to the stacks of baloney.

"But it's never been done," said a worried Miss Beany.

"Until now!" I carried some baloney to the kitchen, cut it into small pieces, mixed it with the hamburger meat, and made one burger. After Miss Beany cooked it, I took a bite. "Hmm. Needs more baloney." So I tried it again. And again, until—

"Here, taste this," I said, handing the burger to Molly. She took a bite. Chewed. Swallowed. Grinned.

"Let me try that," said Miss Beany. She raised the burger closer to her face and sniffed it. Then nibbled on it. Then, while grinning, she took a great big bite.

"And that," I said, "is how to make lemonade."

We all laughed. Then, after mixing the right amount of baloney with the meat, we made over 500 burgers.

"So what do we call them?" asked Molly.

I quickly did the math.

"Perfect," said Molly. She carried a tray to the serving counter. "The kids are going to love baloneyburgers."

"But how about *them*?" asked a nervous Miss Beany. As she stood behind the counter, she pointed with her eyes to the two grumpy-looking people at the front of the lunch line— Principal Hawk, and the Food Inspector!

CHAPTER TWELVE

SURPRISE!

I watched as the stony-faced principal and Food Inspector picked up lunch trays and moved closer. Fortunately, we had everything ready (even without any help from the still sleeping Mrs. Wolf).

"This is like a test for you, isn't it?" I asked Miss Beany.

She nodded nervously.

"And a test for you, Maloney," roared Principal Hawk as he moved in front of me. I placed a baloneyburger on his plate. "Because if whatever this is doesn't taste good, you'll be spending another week in the kitchen."

80

Of course, Miss Beany's punishment for a bad report from the Food Inspector would be even worse. "I could get fired," she told me as we watched the principal and the inspector carry their trays to a nearby table.

DO YOU GET NERVOUS WHEN THE FOOD INSPECTOR EATS THE LUNCH YOU MADE?
YES.

BUT NOT AS NERVOUS AS WHEN HE DOESN'T EAT THE LUNCH I MADE.

GUY MALONEY

Fortunately, the Food Inspector cleared his plate. So did Principal Hawk.

"You think they liked it?" asked a nervous Miss Beany.

"I don't know," I replied, "but I think we're about to find out."

I watched the two men chat for a moment before standing up and walking closer. I looked for a clue as to what they were thinking. But all I saw was—

A blank-faced stare

Principal Hawk's normal angry bulldog expression

"I never thought this would happen," snarled Principal Hawk.

There was a chilly silence.

"What?" I finally asked.

The principal pointed at us, then at the Food Inspector. "He'll tell you."

The Inspector cleared his throat. Then, in a low, buttery voice said, "I am here to inform you that the quality of your food was—"

"Was what?" interrupted a shaky Miss Beany.

The inspector's eyebrows danced upward. "It was excellent!" he said with a smile. "The apple crumb cake was scrumptious. The potato puffs, delightful. And these—"

"They're called baloneyburgers," I said.

"Well, they were creative and tasty."

"Did you hear that, Guy?" asked Molly while patting me on the back. "He likes them!"

"And tell them the best part," said Principal Hawk while flashing a rare smile.

"Because of your achievement, I am presenting you with the 'Clean Plate Award.'" The Inspector pulled a shiny plaque from his briefcase.

It was beautiful

It made me smile.

I moved my hands closer and closer.

"This is for Mrs. Wolf!" snapped Principal Hawk.

"Huh?"

"She's the head cook, the one responsible for this lunch. So she deserves the award."

WHAT?!

I looked across the kitchen at the closed office door. Mrs. Wolf was sleeping, doing nothing, and about to get *our* award. "It's not fair!" I grumbled.

Unfortunately, I couldn't do anything about it. Or could I?

Principal Hawk rubbed his hand on the shiny plaque and grinned. "So where is Mrs. Wolf?" He glanced around, as if surprised she wasn't there.

"She's…she's unavailable," said Miss Beany softly.

"Still working, is she?"

Miss Beany nearly choked.

I nearly exploded. But instead, I thought about what was happening. And I grinned from ear to ear as I came up with a plan. "Come see for yourself," I said. I tugged on the principal's arm and led him to Mrs. Wolf's office.

Then, I opened the door.

THE BARKER

Rockyville Elementary School News

CAUGHT!

Head cook Mrs. Wolf was caught sleeping on the job by Principal Hawk. Still, she tried to convince him she had helped with lunch. "I did some sleepwalking...and some sleepcooking," she explained.

"Baloney!" thundered the angry principal. "You were caught on your chair in your office. And all you were doing was sleep*sitting*!"

BALONEY SCHOOL

Students loved eating the baloneyburger, the newest school menu item. "And after lunch," chuckled Guy Maloney, "everyone at school was full of baloney!"

SURPRISE AWARD

In a shocking surprise, Rockyville Elementary School was awarded the "Clean Plate Award" for Friday's lunch. According to the Food Inspector, the food served (especially the baloneyburger) was delicious.

It was the school's first ever food award. Although Molly Duncan, a student kitchen helper, joked that it was actually a "second" award. "Because after eating a baloneyburger," she said, "everyone wanted a second."

TODAY WAS A SCHOOL CAFETERIA FIRST.

BECAUSE THE LUNCH WON AN AWARD?

BECAUSE THE LUNCH TASTED LIKE FOOD.

GUY MALONEY

CHAPTER THIRTEEN
IT ALL ADDS UP

On Monday, everything was back to normal.
I was in math class, and was working on an idea
for **COMIC GUY** (which Zoe, reluctantly, let
stay in the newspaper).

Everyone laughed. Except, of course, Mr. Crane, who assigned me an extra page of homework problems. Then, for a few minutes, he left the room.

"Can you believe it?" asked Molly.

"Yeah," I said, looking at my extra work. "And it's not fair!"

"I mean about Mrs. Wolf's excuse?"

"What excuse?"

"The excuse she gave Principal Hawk for falling asleep in her office. She blamed it on the math she had to do."

"Which is probably true." I chuckled while faking a yawn. "So what did Principal Hawk do?"

"He exploded."

"And fired her?"

"No. He sentenced her to an even worse punishment."

"Worse than being fired?"

"Yep."

"What?"

Molly's eyes pointed toward the front of the room. Toward the doorway. Toward Mrs. Wolf, who pushed her way in like an angry bear and looked around. Then, she spotted me.

The room grew silent as she stomped down my aisle.

I gulped, because I knew what was coming.

Mrs. Wolf moved closer.

I slouched down in my chair, trying to hide.

She stopped, glared at me, then slammed a math book onto the empty desk next to mine.

"Can you believe it?" she growled. "I've been sentenced to one week in math class."

I watched her plop her chunky body onto the small chair. Then I continued working on a **COMIC GUY** comic strip.

And I smiled.

Because sometimes, life is fair.

CREATING COMIC STRIPS
the COMIC GUY way

Lesson Three: DRAWING FUNNY PICTURES

A funny idea needs a funny picture.

SO HOW DO YOU DRAW A FUNNY PICTURE, GUY?

I GET PAPER, A PENCIL WITH A BIG ERASER, AND...

(A) I **DRAW**. (B) I **SIMPLIFY**. (C) I **EXAGGERATE**.

an (almost) normal Mr. Crane

round eyes

three-finger hands

simple pants and shoes

pointy hair

beak-like nose

small chin

large feet

I DON'T FEEL LIKE MYSELF TODAY, MOLLY.

LET ME GUESS. YOU FEEL LIKE A COMIC STRIP CHARACTER.

HOW DID YOU KNOW?

GUY MALONEY

It doesn't happen by accident. If you want to learn to draw funny pictures, you must do three important things — PRACTICE! PRACTICE! PRACTICE! Get the picture? Good. Now get some paper, a pencil (with a large eraser), and start creating some funny pictures!

Learn more about creating comic strips by reading the lessons found in all the **COMIC GUY** books.

About the Author/Illustrator

Timothy Roland never worked in a school kitchen. But he was a school cook. Because he spent a lot of his school time cooking up ideas for comic strips. . . and then cooking up excuses when he got caught doing it during class.

Today, Timothy cooks up material for **COMIC GUY** at his home in Pennsylvania. His recipe for creating comic strips involves mixing humorous characters into an idea, sprinkling it with silliness, then baking it in his imagination until it's well-done—and funny.

RUN

CLIMB

or TRIP

into all of **COMIC GUY'S** adventures!